This book was first published in 1987 by Bracken Books
a division of Bestseller Publications Ltd
Princess House, 50 Eastcastle Street
London W1N 7AP, England

ISBN 1 85170 123 0

Printed and bound by Times Printers, Singapore

TOWN MOUSE & COUNTRY MOUSE
AND OTHER TALES

RETOLD BY
GERALDINE CARTER

ILLUSTRATED BY
JANE HARVEY

BRACKEN BOOKS
LONDON

Town Mouse and Country Mouse

Once upon a time there were two cousins, a Town Mouse, and a Country Mouse. The Country Mouse lived in a hole directly beneath a grassy bank. In one corner of her little hole stood her bed, made from scrumpled up newspaper and twigs; in another lay her hoard of nuts, and odd bits and pieces.

One day Country Mouse was delighted to receive a visit from her cousin, the Town Mouse. But Town Mouse was rather grumpy after her long trek and squeaked indignantly at her cousin: "Do you really live in a dark little hole, can this be your *real* home?"

Country Mouse was most upset. "It's all my own," she replied, "I've got everything I need here."

"It's fit only for beetles and ants," muttered Town Mouse as she surveyed the little hole. "You've got no idea what it is like in my house. Fine rooms, corridors to race down, each day a feast of crumbs under the dining room table."

"My food is delicious too," interrupted

Country Mouse as she scuttled away to her pantry. "Dear cousin, take a nibble at this fine apple core or perhaps you would prefer to gnaw at one of my rinds of cheese."

"*Rind* did you say? In my house there's a pantry as big as your mouse hole piled high with cheeses – whole ones, holey ones, soft ones, hard ones, smelly ones – you've simply no idea. I'll just munch a few of your nuts," said Town Mouse.

Then she turned to Country Mouse: "Now listen, I simply cannot stay here a moment longer. You must accompany me, *dear* cousin, to my house. You'll soon see how we mice really live."

Off they set through the fields and lanes and came, at last, to the town. "Ordinary houses," muttered Town Mouse as they scurried along, "wait until you see *my* house."

A short time later they came to a grand house. Town Mouse led the way under the door, through the hall and along the passage. Finally they reached the pantry. Country Mouse's whiskers were quivering and twitching with excitement as she spied first a great smoked ham, then piles of apples, and giant cheeses.

Country Mouse scuttled towards the cheese as Town Mouse squeaked: "Keep away, there's a trap that'll snap you in two. Scramble up on the shelf. It's safe there."

Suddenly the door opened: "Quick, hide, it's the cook," whispered Town Mouse, and the two mice scurried behind a great jar of pickles.

"Mice!" muttered the cook. "Puss, puss," he shouted through the open door, "catch those horrors at once, or there will be no supper for you."

The door slammed shut and the great ginger tom leapt onto a shelf. The two mice dived onto the floor to escape and as the cat jumped down he could see Town Mouse's tail disappearing into a hole in the baseboard. But poor Country Mouse was not so lucky. She panicked, and slithered this way and that and the cat pounced on her, let her go, and pounced again. He drove her right up to the open hole but, as he lifted his paw, Country Mouse darted into the hole, safe at last. A few minutes later she peeped out, saw the ginger tom lapping up his saucer of milk, and bolted for the door. She squeezed under it and ran all the way home. She looked around her cosy hole before snuggling down contentedly on her bed of newspaper and twigs. How much better was her own simple home than all the luxuries of town life!

Aladdin

Once upon a time there lived a poor tailor with a son called Aladdin, a lazy young lad who spent all his time idling about the streets. One day a stranger approached him and asked whether he was, by chance, the son of Mustapha. "I am indeed," replied Aladdin, surprised by the stranger's question, "but my father is dead and has been for many years."

On hearing Aladdin's words, the stranger embraced him warmly and patted him on the back: "Wonderful, wonderful, my boy!" he exclaimed, putting his arm around Aladdin's shoulder. "Here I am at last, your long-lost uncle. Please do me a favor . Run and tell your mother I am here. This evening I shall come to dine with her."

Now this stranger was no relation of Aladdin's. He was a famous African magician who wanted Aladdin for his own purposes, as we shall see.

That evening the magician, laden down with wine and fruit, presented himself at Aladdin's house. His poor mother was delighted and believed the magician actually was her long lost brother-in-law. Later that evening, when he learned that Aladdin was an idle rascal who scampered off at the very mention of work, the magician turned to him: "Come, come, boy, no son of my dear departed brother can be left to twiddle his thumbs. There's plenty for a bright young fellow like you to do. Tut, tut." "Indeed," he went on, waving his arms about, "I've got just the trade for you! I'll set you up in a shop, stock it with exotic fruits and spices and in no time you'll be the smartest shopkeeper in town." Aladdin and his mother couldn't believe their luck and when, in the morning, the magician appeared with a fine suit of clothes for Aladdin their happiness was complete.

The following day the magician asked Aladdin to join him on an important expedition. Then he led Aladdin out through the city gates right into the heart of the countryside. In the heat of the day they stopped to eat some bread and, as they munched away, the magician pointed to the steep mountains facing them and told Aladdin that there the expedition would end. On and on they walked and when, at last, they reached the two mountains, divided by a narrow valley, the magician became very agitated and shouted at Aladdin: "Gather up some sticks, my boy. We shall light a fire

and then go about our business."
Aladdin did as he was told and
watched the magician light his
fire. Then the magician sprinkled
some strange smelling powder
over the flames, murmuring as he
did so. Suddenly the earth started
to shake and tremble; a great
gashing hole opened before him.
Aladdin was terrified. He could
hardly bear to look at the empty
hole. Turning, he started to run
away but the magician grasped
his arm and pointed to a square
flat stone with a brass ring
embedded in it: "Beneath this
stone lies treasure. It is yours,
no one else may touch it.
Stop this shivering and
shaking and pull that ring in
front of you."

Aladdin lifted up the stone
without difficulty. There,
before him, lay a flight of
uneven stone steps. The
magician, in an excitable mood,
shouted: "Get down there and at
the foot of the steps you will find
an open door leading into three
vast underground halls. Don't
touch anything or you will
instantly die. These halls lead
out into a garden of trees laden
with fruit. Walk out towards the
lighted lamp. Pour its oil onto
the path and return to me with
this lamp." Then from his finger

he pulled a jewelled ring and presented it to Aladdin.

Well, Aladdin did exactly as he was told, stopping only to pick a little fruit on the way which he stuffed into his pockets. At the mouth of the cave he called out: "Uncle, I've got the lamp!"

"Give it to me, give it to me," shouted the magician impatiently.

"Just wait now, Uncle," teased Aladdin clasping the lamp tightly in his arms. The thwarted magician flew into a violent rage, chucked the rest of his powder on to the dying flames of the fire, muttering angrily. At once the stone above Aladdin's head rolled back into place.

It was dark, very dark in the musty cave and for two days Aladdin groped around in the black hole. At last he rubbed the ring on his finger. A large and frightening genie appeared in a burst of light, and piped out in a thin, silvery voice: "I am the slave of the ring. What do you want." "Let me out of here," gasped Aladdin. At once the stone rolled back and Aladdin scrambled out. Soon he was on his way back to the city. Entering his house he ran to his mother and showed her the lamp. As he took the fruit from his pocket, he told her what had happened. "Sell the lamp and buy some food for us," Aladdin then advised her, and she set about cleaning the lamp. At once a hideous genie appeared.

"What do you want?" it squawked.

"Food, food. Fetch me something to eat!" Aladdin replied, realizing that the lamp, too, possessed magical powers. In a flash, the genie was back, this time with a silver bowl, twelve silver plates containing rich meats, two silver cups, and two bottles of wine.

And for some years Aladdin and his mother lived by the magical powers of the lamp and the gold ring. Then, one day, Aladdin happened to catch a glimpse of the Sultan's daughter through a crack in the palace wall. So beautiful was she, he fell in love with her instantly. That evening Aladdin begged his mother to present herself to the Sultan and to ask him to give his daughter's hand in marriage to Aladdin.

And so Aladdin's mother found herself carrying the magic fruits from the enchanted garden to the Sultan's palace. After a week waiting for an audience she presented the dazzling jewels to the Sultan and made her request. Deeply moved, he turned to her and said: "So great is the love of your son for my daughter, so dazzling the jewels he has bestowed upon me, he is indeed worthy to be my son-in-law." But one of his listening courtiers persuaded the Sultan to postpone the marriage for three months; he wanted his own son to marry the princess. Aladdin's mother was, therefore, bidden to return to the palace with her son three months hence.

Some weeks later Aladdin's mother learned that the Sultan's daughter was to marry the son of the courtier that very day. Aladdin was beside himself with grief. He picked up the lamp, rubbed it, and commanded the genie to bring the bride and bridegroom to him. That night their bed was transported to his room. The bridegroom was forced out into the bitter cold while Aladdin explained to the terrified princess that she was really his wife, promised to him by her father. At dawn the shivering bridegroom and the Sultan's daughter were transported back to the palace.

The Sultan was alarmed at the sight of his pale and miserable daughter. At last she related the strange story to him. "A dream, a dream," her father assured her, but that night the same thing happened, and again the following night. The courtier's son said he would rather die than spend another such fearful night, and asked to be separated from the Sultan's daughter. His wish was granted, and there was an end of feasting and rejoicing.

When the three months were over Aladdin sent his mother to remind the Sultan of his promise: "Good woman, a Sultan must remember his promises, but tell your son to send me forty gold bowls brimful of jewels.

And so Aladdin summoned the genie and, in a flash, forty servants stood before him. As they set out to the palace, two by two, carrying on their heads gold basins filled with sparkling jewels, crowds formed to witness the procession. The Sultan was beside himself with delight: "Good woman, return and tell your son that I wait for him with open arms." Aladdin, when he heard this, summoned the genie and requested a magnificent horse, twenty servants, a gown embroidered with gold thread, and ten thousand pieces of gold.

When the Sultan set eyes on Aladdin, he embraced him and nodded as Aladdin told him that he would build a palace for his princess. At home, once more, Aladdin turned to the genie: "Build me a palace of the finest

marble, set with jasper, agate, and other precious stones."

The very next day Aladdin's palace stood in all its splendor overlooking the town.

But far away in Africa the magician remembered Aladdin and by his magic arts discovered what had happened. He vowed to get hold of the lamp and returned to the old city to carry out his plan. The scheming fellow wasted no time in buying a dozen copper lamps which he marched with to the palace, crying: "New lamps for old! New lamps for old!" The princess was enthralled by this idea and told her servant to fetch Aladdin's old lamp from a corner of his study. Together they presented it to the magician in exchange for a fine new lamp. The magician snatched the magic lamp and hurried away.

Through the city gates the magician ran and on to a deserted encampment where he remained till nightfall. Then he pulled the lamp out of his sack and rubbed it vigorously. The genie popped up and at the magician's command carried him, together with the palace and the princess, to a lonely, sandswept plain in North Africa.

The following morning the Sultan happened to look out of the window towards Aladdin's palace. He could not believe his eyes. Nothing! Nothing at all! He called for his chief courtier who protested that Aladdin was an enchanter. The Sultan, on hearing these words ordered his cavalry to set out and to capture Aladdin.

That evening Aladdin was brought before the Sultan who ordered his head to be cut off. And, as the Sultan shouted: "Where is my daughter – where is your palace?" Aladdin realized what had come to pass. He begged time to find the princess. "Forty days I will give you and if you fail in your task then you will certainly lose your head."

Aladdin was quite distraught. After two days spent wandering about in a dazed state he was so exhausted his hands began to tremble. He looked down at them and the gleaming stone in his ring caught his eye. The ring! Suddenly he remembered. He rubbed his finger hard and amidst a puff of smoke the genie appeared: "Take me to my palace and set me down under my wife's window," Aladdin pleaded.

He fell into a deep sleep and awoke under the princess' window just as her servant was opening the window. The girl immediately informed the princess who ran out to greet him. For a while they were overcome with joy but Aladdin did not forget their danger: "Quick, tell me,

what has become of the old lamp in the corner of my dressing room."

"The African magician who is trying to win my affection carries it about with him," replied the princess sorrowfully.

"Trust me," Aladdin said, "for I must get the lamp. Persuade the magician to dine with you and prepare to put on your most splendid gown. I will return shortly and tell you what you must do."

When Aladdin returned having purchased a particular powder in the town, he gave the princess her instructions. In the evening, the magician was astonished to see the princess dressed so sumptuously and pleasantly surprised to hear her declare that, since Aladdin must be dead, she would welcome his company. "Pray let us celebrate this joyous occasion," she declared as she handed him a goblet in which she had placed Aladdin's powder. He raised it to his lips, took a hearty sip and fell down dead, quite dead.

And now Aladdin lost no time in recovering the lamp and in summoning the genie to carry the palace and all therein back to their own city. The following day the Sultan glanced sorrowfully out of his window. Lo and behold there stood Aladdin's palace as if nothing at all had happened. He hastened to greet his daughter and from her learned of the evil intentions of the magician and of his timely death. At once the Sultan proclaimed a week of celebration and feasting for all his peoples. Some years later Aladdin became Sultan and reigned wisely for many years, encouraging his subjects in the ways of hard work, for he never forgot his own idle youth.

The Little Mermaid

Once upon a time far out to sea where the water is as blue as the brightest cornflower and as clear as the purest crystal, there dwelt the Mermen, and in the deepest part of the ocean lay the palace of the Merman King. The king's palace was surrounded by the most wonderful trees and plants, its walls formed of coral, and its long pointed windows carved from the clearest amber. Its roof was tiled with mussel shells, a gleaming pearl set in each one.

The Merman King had for many years been a widower and he had six daughters who were all lovely, but the youngest daughter was the prettiest of all. Her skin was as soft and delicate as a rose petal and her eyes as blue as the depths of the sea. Like all mermaids she possessed, in place of legs and feet, a fish's tail.

Nothing pleased the youngest princess more than to hear about the world of human beings living above the sea. She listened intently to her grandmother's stories of towns and people, animals and flowers. "When you are fifteen you will be allowed to rise up from the sea and sit on the rocks in the moonlight, and look at the big ships sailing by, and you too will see the woods and towns."

But there were five whole years to wait before she could rise from the bottom of the sea. Many a night the little mermaid stood by the open windows and looked up through the dark blue water, which the fish lashed with their tails and fins, and gazed at the far-off moon and the stars.

By now the eldest princess had reached her fifteenth birthday and could venture above the water. When she returned she had hundreds of things to tell them, but the most delightful of all, she said, was to lie in the moonlight on a sandbank and gaze at the large town close to the shore, where the lights twinkled like hundreds

of stars. How eagerly the young princess listened to her sister's tales. When later in the evening she stood at the open window and looked up through the dark blue water, she thought of the big town with all its noise and bustle, and fancied that she could even hear church bells ringing.

The next year the second sister rose to the surface of the sea just as the sun was setting on the horizon. It was, she declared, the most beautiful sight that she had ever seen. The sky was like gold, the clouds floated in red and violet splendor over her head and a flock of wild swans flew like a long white veil over the water towards the setting sun; she swam towards the sun, but it sank, and all the rosy light on cloud and water faded away.

When it was the third sister's turn she ventured up a river and looked at the beautiful green vine-clad hills and saw palaces and grand houses peeping through splendid woods. In a tiny bay she found a group of little children running about naked and paddling in the water. She called to them but they were frightened and ran away.

The fourth sister was not so bold; she stayed in the remotest part of the ocean where she could see for miles and miles around her, and stare at the sky above which looked, she thought, like a great glass dome.

Now it was the fifth sister's turn. It was winter and the sea was green with large icebergs floating on its surface. They looked like pearls, she said, with the most wonderful shapes and sparkled like diamonds. She sat down to rest on a floating iceberg but as evening approached the sky became overcast and a storm erupted. She listened to the thunder and watched the blue lightning flash in zigzags down on the shining sea.

At last it was the little mermaid's turn and through the water she rose, as lightly and airily as a bubble. The sun had just set as her head emerged above the water, the clouds still lighted with a rose and golden splendor and the air mild and fresh. A large three-masted ship lay close by. There was music and singing on board and as darkness fell hundreds of gaily colored lanterns were lighted.

The little mermaid swam right up to the cabin windows and looked through at the crowds of gaily-dressed people. She gazed at the handsome young prince in whose honor these festivities were taking place. Suddenly hundreds of fireworks erupted and so frightened her that she dived under the

water. As she rose again it seemed as though all the stars of heaven were falling in showers around about her. Great suns whirled round, fire-fish hung in the blue air. It grew late but still the little mermaid was mesmerized by the ship and the beautiful prince.

Suddenly a violent storm blew up and the little mermaid found herself buffeted by waves. The ship heaved and listed in the angry sea. Black waves rose like mountains and broke over its decks, snapping the main mast like a reed.

As it split apart the little mermaid saw that the prince was drowning. She swam towards him. He was unconscious as she held his head above the water and allowed the waves to drive them hither and thither throughout the long night. At daybreak she could see the shoreline covered with beautiful green woods. She swam towards it and placed the prince on a strip of fine white sand, with his head in the warm sunshine.

Bells now began to ring in a great white temple by the shore and a number of young girls came out into an orchard of orange and lemon trees. When the girls saw the prince they were frightened but soon he revived and they flocked around him. He never looked towards the sea where the little mermaid was resting and she thought he had forgotten her. The most beautiful of the girls led the prince back into the white temple and the little mermaid dived sorrowfully into the water and made her way home.

Many an evening the little mermaid rose from the sea to the inlet where she had left the prince. The fruit in the garden ripened, and the snow melted on the mountain tops, but in all that time she never saw the prince again.

At last she could bear it no longer and she told her sisters about the prince and the coast where she had left him. One of the mermaids knew the country where the prince lived and the following day the mermaids rose from the water in a long line, just in front of the prince's palace: a palace of glistening yellow stone, with great marble staircases. Through clear glass they could see a splendid hall adorned with silk hangings and in its center lay a large fountain throwing jets of spray towards a sunlit glass dome.

Often in the evenings the little mermaid would swim close to the land and watch the young prince walking in the gardens or sailing his boat. She longed more and more to live with people.

"If men are not drowned," she asked her grandmother one day, "do they live for ever?" "They die too," the old lady answered "and their lives are much shorter than ours. We may live here for three hundred years, but when we cease to exist, we become foam on the water. They have immortal souls which live for ever."

"So I will die and become foam on the sea. Is there nothing I can do to gain an immortal soul?"

"Only if a human being should bestow on you all his love would you then gain an immortal soul."

"I would give my three hundred years to be a human being for one day, and to have a share in the heavenly kingdom," she said sadly.

It was then that the little mermaid decided to visit the sorceress whose abode lay in a grim and desolate part of the sea-bed. As she passed

through a writhing mass of water snakes she was almost choked by slimy weeds of a dank sea forest, and finally she came to a house built of bones. As she swam in the sorceress said: "I know very well why you have come. You want to get rid of your fish's tail, and have two stumps to walk upon so that the young prince may fall in love with you. I will make you a potion and before sunrise you must swim ashore with it. Drink it on the beach; your tail will divide and shrivel up and form into what men call legs. But remember, you can never be a mermaid again and if you do not succeed in winning the prince's love you will only turn into sea foam."

"I will do it," said the mermaid, pale as death.

"But you will have to pay me, too," said the witch. "I will have your voice in return for my precious potion."

"But if you take my voice," said the little mermaid, "what have I left?"

"Why, your beauty, and your eyes full of expression; with these you ought to be able to bewitch a human heart. Have you lost courage?"

"Let it be done then," said the little mermaid.

The witch scoured her cauldron with a bundle of snakes, and piled in the ingredients for the magic brew. As it started to bubble it made strange sounds like crocodiles' weeping. At last the potion was ready. "There it is," said the witch as she cut off the tongue of the little mermaid.

Later that evening, the mermaid rose up through the dark blue water, and saw the moon shine bright and clear over the prince's palace. Slowly she drank the burning, stinging potion and lost consciousness. She awoke to find the handsome young prince fixing his coal black eyes on her. Who was she, he asked, and how did she get there? She looked at him tenderly and with such a sad expression in her eyes that he took her by the hand and led her into the palace. The potion had worked its magic and as she walked she glanced down at her new legs and feet and felt that she was treading on spikes.

In the palace she was clothed in the costliest silks and muslins. All who saw her admired her grace and beauty but the little mermaid was neither able to sing nor speak. Everywhere the prince went she followed and he loved her as one loves a good sweet child.

"Am I not dearer to you than any of the others?" the little mermaid's eyes seemed to say.

He appeared to understand what she was trying to say: "Yes you are the dearest one to me," he told her, "for you have the best heart of them all. You are like a young girl I once saw but whom I never expect to see again. I was on board a ship which was wrecked and she saved my life. She was the only person I could love in this world."

One day it was announced that the prince was to be married to the beautiful daughter of a neighboring king,   and a splendid ship was fitted out for the journey. "I must go and see the beautiful princess, my parents demand that, but they will never force me to bring her home as my bride; I can never love her."

"You are not frightened of the sea, my beautiful, silent child?" he asked as they stood together on the ship's deck. When the ship entered the harbor of the neighboring king, church bells rang and trumpets sounded from every lofty tower. There were balls and receptions and when at last the princess made her entrance the little mermaid recognized at once her exquisite beauty.

"It is you who saved me when I lay almost lifeless on the beach," the prince gasped as he saw her.

Their wedding day was set and the little mermaid felt as if her heart would break. As church bells pealed, and heralds rode through the town proclaiming the wedding the little mermaid, dressed in silk and gold, stood holding the bride's train. That same evening the bride and bridegroom went on board ship to the sound of cannons firing and, as darkness grew, colored lamps were hung throughout the ship and sailors danced merrily on deck. The little mermaid knew that soon she would be dead. As she looked overboard she saw her sisters rise from the water, their faces pale as her own, their beautiful long hair no longer floating on the breeze.

"We have given it to the witch to obtain her help, so that you may not die tonight; she has given us a knife, here it is. Plunge it into the prince's heart and you will once more become a mermaid and live out your three hundred years." But when she saw him sleeping peacefully she could not harm him. She kissed his fair brow and threw the knife far out among the waves.

As the sun rose from the sea the little mermaid saw hundreds of ethereal beings floating overhead, their voices so spirit-like no human ear could hear them. Light as bubbles they drifted through the air and suddenly the little mermaid realized that her form had become like theirs.

"You have come to join the daughters of the air!" said one, "a mermaid has no undying soul, her eternal life depends upon an unknown power but by their own good deeds they may create one for themselves. We bring cool breezes to the tropics, we scatter the scent of flowers over the earth, and when, for three hundred years, we have labored to do all the good in our power we gain an undying soul and take part in the everlasting joys of mankind."

On board ship all was again life and bustle, and she watched as the prince with his lovely bride searched for her; they looked sadly at the bubbling foam, as if they knew that she had thrown herself into the waves. Unseen she kissed the bride on her brow, smiled at the prince and rose aloft with other spirits of the air to the rosy clouds which sailed above.

The

Emperor's New Clothes

Once upon a time there lived an Emperor who cared about nothing but his splendid clothes. He had a wardrobe as big as a ballroom, and there he spent all his spare time. He rarely left his wardrobe except to show off his clothes.

The Emperor's wardrobe was famous all over the world, and tailors were always sure of finding a job at the palace – it was considered a great honor to add to his magnificent wardrobe. One day, however, two swindlers came to the Emperor as he was trying on a new suit with purple zig-zags. These swindlers announced that they were weavers, and asked the Emperor if he desired to see proof of their skill. Apparently they could weave the world's most beautiful clothes, with astounding colors and marvellous shifting patterns. Not only that, but a suit of clothes made from their cloth would seem invisible to anyone who was dull or unfit for high office. The Emperor was dumbfounded at the thought of acquiring clothes that could also become invisible.

"Imagine! With splendid garments like that I could easily discover which of my Councillors are worthy of their office."

The two swindlers were set work at once, and the Emperor left orders that they should be given as many fine materials as they wished. And what materials they demanded! The finest silks and velvets in every color of the rainbow, along with enough gold and silver thread to sew one hundred suits. All of these materials the swindlers bundled into their own bags while they worked away at the empty looms. The Emperor insisted that no-one should disturb the weavers until they had finished but finally he grew impatient and sent his wisest minister to inspect the work.

As the minister entered the room, he saw the swindlers working hard at their looms. But, as far as he could see, the looms were empty!

"Do come closer," invited one of the swindlers. "Have you come to see how we're getting on?"

"Er. . . yes," stammered the poor minister. "The Emperor himself has sent me."

On hearing this, both swindlers eagerly begged him to give them his honest opinion on the material they were weaving. The minister stared and stared at the looms but he still could see nothing. "Why, I must be unfit for my royal office!" he thought, much astonished. "I must never, *ever* let the Emperor know, or he will dispense with my services and banish me to the country."

So the minister smiled at the swindlers and assured them that the material was all that could be desired. Then he hurried off to inform the Emperor that the fabulous new suit of clothing was coming along well. A few days later the Emperor again became anxious to see how his clothes were getting on; this time he sent one of his most faithful chancellors.

"My goodness gracious me," muttered the chancellor to himself as he entered the room, "these looms are bare!"

He peered through his spectacles at the empty looms then he rushed out of the room, and ran straight to the Emperor to praise the material. "Your majesty *must* make these wonderful men Royal Weavers," he declared.

At this, the Emperor became so curious that he decided to inspect the weavers himself. So, accompanied by several court officials, he marched through the palace, until he reached the weavers' room. He strode forward, impatient to see his new clothes.

But the Emperor himself could not see anything on the looms!

"This is tragic," he moaned to himself. "Whatever shall I do? If I admit in front of all my officials that I can see nothing, I will be the laughing-stock of

my Kingdom.
Oh how unfair life is!"

The Emperor almost burst into tears in his distress. But then he thought that nobody would know how unfit he was to be Emperor if he let them think that he really could see the clothes. "Breathtaking! Astounding! Magnificent!" he cried out. "Such originality! How do *you* feel about them, my friends?" he asked his silent officials.

"Exquisite!" murmured one of the Chancellors.

Everyone looked at the looms; but not a single person was brave enough to admit that he could see no cloth.

"I shall wear these clothes in the great procession next week," announced the Emperor grandly. "All my people will be overjoyed to see me wearing them at last; they are the talk of the Kingdom."

So that week the swindlers sat up late every night, pretending to complete the clothes. All day they cut and sewed, snipping at thin air, and sewing with threadless needles; every visitor heaped praise on the work of the swindlers.

At last, the day of the procession arrived. The sun was shining brightly and, at six o'clock in the morning, the streets were already lined with impatient people. The Emperor hurried to the swindlers and asked if the new clothes were ready.

"Why, yes indeed, your Majesty," replied the swindlers. "They are here, waiting for you to put them on."

"Well.... yes... um... er... thank-you," stuttered the Emperor, still hardly able to believe that the clothes were invisible to him. "They're more beautiful than ever."

Then the Emperor took off his pink satin nightgown. The swindlers pretended to help him on with the new clothes. An old

Councillor stood by, shaking his head in mock amazement and marvelling at the perfect fit. Soon everybody in the room was following his example, shaking their heads like dodos and clucking in astonishment. At last the Emperor was ready. He turned round and round several times in front of the mirror to give the appearance of admiring the clothes. Then the Emperor's most honored officials pretended to pick up his train.

Crowds were shouting for the Emperor, and all the people were craning their necks and standing on tip-toe in an effort to be the first to see the famous clothes. The Emperor strode into view, and suddenly, after a moment of silence, everyone began cheering and praising the weavers, who were also in the procession. All the people started to admire the non-existent clothes at the top of their voices, for they did not want to look like fools. But one little girl, bored by hearing her parents go on and on about the magnificence of the colors, and the delicacy of the cloth, said loudly: "But he hasn't got anything on!"

"*What* did you say? *He hasn't got anything on?* Why, you silly little girl, of course our Emperor has got something on!" gasped her father.

"Shhhh! hissed the girl's mother. "The neighbors might hear!"

But the neighbors *had* heard. Gradually the little girl's words were whispered among the crowd until everyone had heard them. Finally all the people cried out together: "*But the Emperor hasn't got anything on!*"

The Emperor heard them clearly, and realized how he had been tricked. Furiously he turned on the swindlers, but they had slipped away.

"There is nothing I can do," he thought miserably. "I will simply have to go through with the procession now."

So the Emperor marched on, more upright than ever, and the officials continued to hold up the invisible train.

The Princess and the Pea

Once upon a time, in a far-off kingdom there lived a prince, and he wanted a princess, but then she must be a *real* princess. He traveled right round the world to find one, but there was always something wrong. There were plenty of princesses, short ones, tall ones, fat ones, thin ones, but whether they were real princesses he had great difficulty in discovering. There was always something which was not quite right about them. So at last he returned home again, and he was very sad because he wanted a real princess so badly.

One evening there was a terrible storm; it thundered, with great flashes of lightning, and the rain poured down in torrents. Indeed it was a fearful night.

In the middle of the storm somebody knocked at the palace gate, and the old King himself went to open it.

It was a princess who stood outside, but she was in a terrible state from the rain and the storm. The water streamed out of her hair and her clothes, it ran in at the top of her shoes and out at the heel, but she said that she was a real princess and she had heard that the prince would only marry a real princess and no-one else.

"Well we shall soon see if that is true," thought the old Queen, but she said nothing. She went into the bedroom, took all the bedclothes off and laid a pea on the bedstead; then she took twenty mattresses and piled them on the top of the pea, and then twenty feather beds on the top of the mattresses. This was where the princess was to sleep that night. In the morning they asked her how she had slept.

"Oh terribly badly!" said the Princess. "I have hardly closed my eyes the whole night!

Heaven knows what was in the bed. I seemed to be lying upon some hard thing, and my whole body is black and blue this morning. It is terrible!"

They saw at once that she must be a real princess, after all she had felt the pea through twenty mattresses and twenty feather beds. Nobody but a real princess could have such a delicate skin.

So the prince took her to be his wife, for now he was sure that he had found a real princess, and the pea was put into the Museum, where it may still be seen if no one has stolen it.

Tom Tit Tot

Once upon a time there was a woman and one day she baked five pies. But when they came out of the oven the crusts were rock hard. So she said to her daughter: "Daughter, put those pies on the shelf, and leave them there a little, and they'll be all right."

But the girl said to herself, "Well, what's the use of that. I'll eat them up now." And she set to work and ate them all up.

When evening came the woman said: "Go and get one of those pies. I'm sure the crusts will be soft now." The girl looked and found nothing but the empty dishes. Back she came and said: "No, they are not soft yet."

"Not one of them," said the mother.

"No, not one of them," said the daughter.

"Well, whether they are soft or not," said the mother, "I'll have one for supper."

"But you can't, if they are not soft," protested the girl.

"But I can," said she. "Go and bring the best of them."

"Best or worst," said the girl, "I've eaten them all up, so you can't have any."

Well, the woman was wholly beaten, and she took her spinning wheel to the door to spin, and as she spun she sang:

"My daughter has eaten five, five pies today,
My daughter has eaten five, five pies today."

Walking down the street at that very moment was the king himself and when he heard her sing he stopped and said: "What was that you were singing, my good woman?"

The woman was ashamed to let him hear all about her daughter's greed, so she sang instead:

"My daughter has spun five, five skeins today,
My daughter has spun five, five skeins today."

"My stars!" said the king, "I've never heard of any one who could do that. Look here, I wish for a wife, and I'll marry your daughter. But," he added, "eleven months out of the year she shall have all she desires but the last month of the year she must spin five skeins every day.

otherwise I shall kill her."

The woman agreed; for she knew what a grand marriage that would be. And as for the five skeins, well, when the time came, they would think of something.

So they were married and the girl had everything she desired. But when the twelfth month drew near, she began to worry about the skeins. But not a word did the king say.

However, on the last day of the eleventh month he took her to a room she had never seen before. "Now, my dear," he said, "you'll be shut in here tomorrow with some food and some flax, and if you haven't spun five skeins by night, off will go your head." And he left her in the room with nothing but a spinning-wheel and a stool.

The girl was terrified and started to cry for she had never even learned how to spin. Suddenly there was a bang and a puff of smoke and the next thing she saw was a small black imp with a long tail walking through the door: "What are you crying for?" it asked.

"Well," she said, "it won't do any harm to tell you, it won't do any good either," and she told the imp all about the pies, and the skeins, and everything.

"Look," said the small black imp, "I shall come to your window every morning, take away the flax, and bring it back spun at night."

"What's your pay?" she asked.

The small black imp looked out of the corner of its eyes, and said: "Three attempts you shall have nightly to guess my name, and if you haven't guessed it before the month is up, you shall be mine."

Well, every day the flax and the food were brought, and every day the small black imp came morning and evening. She never managed to guess its name.

On the last day but one the king came in and said: "Well, my dear, you are progressing so well I've decided to dine here with you tonight."

As they ate their supper he began to laugh.

"What is it?" said she.

"Why," said he, "I was out hunting today, and I got to a place in the wood I had never seen before. I heard a sort of humming in an old chalk-pit, so I got off my horse and took a look. Well, what should be there but the funniest little black imp you ever saw. It had a little spinning-wheel, and was spinning like fury, and twirling its tail. And as it spun, it sang:

"Nimmy, nimmy not, my name's Tom Tit Tot."

When the girl heard this, she could have jumped for joy, but she didn't say a word.

Next day the small black imp looked very full of malice when it came for the flax. "What's my name?" it said.

"Is it Solomon?" said she, pretending to be afraid.

"No it isn't," it said, coming farther into the room.

"Is it Zebedee?" said she.

"No, it isn't," said the imp, laughing and twirling its tail so fast that you could scarcely see it. But now she looked at it and pointing her finger at it, said:

"Nimmy, nimmy not, your name's Tom Tit Tot."

When the imp heard her, it shrieked frightfully, and flew away into the dark, and she never saw it again.

The Ugly Duckling

It was summertime. The wheat was golden, the oats still green, and
the hay lay stacked in the rich, low-lying meadows where the stork
was marching about on his long red legs. In the sunniest spot stood
an old mansion overlooking a deep lake, and great fern leaves
stretched from the walls of the house right
down to the water's edge; some were so tall
that a small child could stand upright under
them. Buried in amongst the leaves was a

duck, sitting on her nest of eggs. At last one egg after another began to crack, and the chicks started poking their heads out.

"Quack! quack!" said the mother, "I suppose you are all here now? No! I declare the biggest egg is still there. How long is this going to continue then?" she said as she settled herself back on the nest once more.

Finally the big egg cracked. "Cheep, cheep!" said the young one as he tumbled out.

"Oh, what a monstrous big duckling," exclaimed his mother, "none of the others looked like that."

The day was a gloriously fine one and the sun shone brightly on all all the green fern leaves, as mother duck led her new family down to the lake. *Splash!* Into the water she sprang, and one duckling after another plopped in after her. Immediately the water dashed over their heads, but up they came and floated about quite beautifully; even the big ugly grey one swam about with them.

Next she took them into the farmyard where they witnessed a

fearful fight, for two families of ducks were squabbling over the head of an eel. In the end the cat captured it. "That's how things go in this world," said the mother duck, and she licked her bill, for she would have loved to gobble up the eel's head herself.

The other ducks were not happy with the new invasion. "Just look what we have to put up with, as if there were not enough of us about already. Oh dear! look at that ugly duckling," one of them muttered as he flew down and bit him in the neck.

"Let him be," said the mother; "he is doing no harm."

But the poor duckling was made fun of by ducks and hens alike. "He is too big," they all said; and the indignant turkey cock puffed himself up like a vessel in full sail till he became quite red in the face. The poor duckling was at his wits' end, he did not know which way to turn. Every day things grew worse and worse. The duckling was chased and hustled, bitten by the ducks and pecked by the hens. Even his brothers and sisters abused him and jeered at him: "If only the cat could get hold of you, you hideous object!"

At last he could stand it no longer. Off he ran straight over the hedge where he so

frightened the little birds they all disappeared. "This is because I am so ugly," thought the poor duckling. On and on he ran until he came to a great marsh where the wild ducks lived. Tired and miserable he stayed there the whole night long without moving. In the morning he hobbled towards a tumbledown little cottage where an old woman lived with her cat and her hen.

"What on earth is that?" said the old woman. Her sight was so bad she mistook him for a large duck. "This is a capital find; now at last I shall have duck's eggs."

The old woman's cat liked to lord it over the duckling and bossed him about whenever she saw fit.

"Do you ever lay eggs?" she asked.

"No," said the duckling quietly.

"Will you have the goodness then to stop all those quacking noises you make!" snapped the cat.

"Can you arch your back, purr, or give off sparks?" asked the cat another time.

"No," said the duckling sadly.

"Then you'd better shut your beak when sensible people are talking."

And so the duckling spent most of his time alone in a corner. One day he found himself longing for the waters of the lake.

He simply had to tell the hen. "What on earth possesses you," she clucked, "haven't you anything else to think about? Lay some eggs or take to purring, and you will soon stop these ridiculous thoughts. You are an idiot; there is no pleasure in having you around."

"I absolutely must go out into the wide world," said the duckling sadly. So back he went to the lakes where every living creature shunned him because of his ugliness.

Autumn came, the leaves in the woods turned brown and red, and the clouds hung heavy with snow and hail. One evening, as the sun was setting in wintry splendor, a flock of large birds appeared; the duckling had never seen anything so beautiful as these dazzling white creatures with their long slender necks. While he was watching, they uttered a peculiar cry, spread out their magnificent wings and flew away from that cold region in the direction of open seas and warmer lands. As they rose high in the sky the ugly little duckling became strangely uneasy. He spun round and round and round in the water like a wheel, craning his neck up into the air in an effort to follow the snow white birds. He did not know what they were, but he felt drawn towards them as he had never before been drawn towards anything else.

Winter was bitterly cold and the duckling was obliged to swim about in the water to stop it from freezing over. Every night the hole in which he swam became smaller and smaller and, in the end, the water froze so hard he found himself stuck fast in the ice.

Early the following morning a farmer rescued the duckling and carried him home. The farmer's children wanted to play with him, but the duckling feared they would abuse him, and in his fright he knocked over the milk pan. Milk spurted out all over the room. In panic, the duckling flew hither and thither knocking over everything in sight. The farmer's wife screamed, the children chased after him and the duckling flew out of the barn door into the snow-covered bushes.

When spring came the duckling raised his wings and found that they flapped with much greater strength than before. Soon he could fly and one day he landed in a large garden where the apple trees were in full blossom, and the air was scented with lilacs. Just in front of him were three beautiful white swans swimming lightly over the water. At once the duckling recognized the majestic birds he had seen last

autumn: "I will fly to them. They might peck me to pieces because I am so ugly but it won't matter; better to risk being killed by them than to be snapped at by ducks, pecked at by hens, or spurned by every living creature."

So he flew into the water and swam towards the stately swans who darted towards him, their feathers ruffled. As they did so, he looked down into the transparent water and saw his own image reflected, but he could see that he was no longer a clumsy dark grey bird, ugly and ungainly; now he was himself a swan! The big swans greeted him and stroked him with their bills. As they were doing so some little children came to the water's edge and threw corn and pieces of bread into the water. The smallest one cried out: "There is a new one!" And they clapped their hands and danced about and exclaimed that the new one was the prettiest of all; he was so young and handsome.

He felt quite shy and hid his head under his wing; he did not know what to think; he was so happy. He thought of how he had been pursued and scorned, and now they were saying that he was the most beautiful of all. The lilacs bent their boughs into the water before him, and the bright sun was warm and cheering, and he rustled his feathers and raised his slender neck aloft. Never in all his life before had he dreamt of so much happiness.

Chantecleer and Partlet

Once upon a time, in a tiny cottage near a clump of shady trees, there lived a poor widow with her two daughters.

In her yard the widow kept a splendid cock, called Chantecleer. This cock had a most remarkable voice; in all the kingdom Chantecleer had no equal. His voice was merrier than the church organ, louder than the loudest town hall clock, and, indeed, with his crowing he kept time as well as any clock. Not only was Chantecleer blessed with a splendid voice but he was also a most handsome fellow. His feathers shone like burnished gold and his comb, bright orange, was shaped like a crenelated castle wall, and stood up proud and tall. His beak glowed and his feet were of the brightest yellow.

For companionship Chantecleer had seven hens, the fairest of whom was called Partlet.

One morning at daybreak, as Chantecleer was sitting on his perch inside the widow's house, with Partlet at his side and other hens nearby, he started making the most hideous noises, groaning like a man in the middle of a bad dream.

Partlet enquired: "What ever is wrong with you, Chantecleer? Why do you make such a dreadful noise?"

Chantecleer answered: "Please do not take offence, Partlet. I dreamed that I was strutting out in our yard when I saw, among the weeds a hound-like beast who would have killed me stone dead. His coat was not

quite yellow, not quite red, and both his ears and tail were tipped with black. His eye was fierce and fiery and he fixed me with such a look I felt that I would die of fear."

"For shame! What a faint-hearted fellow you are," Partlet burst out. "I cannot love a coward like you. Shame on you!" And so Chantecleer was forced to shrug off his fears and soon he had forgotten all about his terrible dream.

But one day, as Partlet was enjoying a sand bath and Chantecleer was singing to her, he caught sight of a butterfly among the grass. The butterfly swooped down and, as it did so, Chantecleer saw the fox he had encountered in his dream crouching low among the grass.

"Cawcaw" cried Chantecleer immediately turning away in terror.

"Where are you going, kind sir," enquired the fox, "surely you are not afraid of me, your friend? I have come on this visit especially to hear you sing. I believe that you have a voice as fine as any angel. Indeed, I have never heard anyone sing better except your own father whose voice was both loud and lordly. Show me, dear fellow, that your voice is the equal of your famous father's".

Chantecleer, delighted to hear such praise from the mouth of the fox, began to beat his wings. He stood on tiptoe, stretched up his neck, shut his eyelids tight and began to crow in a most lordly fashion. But, after he had sung only a few notes, the fox seized him by the throat and ran off towards his den.

Seeing the plight of poor Chantecleer the hens set up a piteous wail and the widow and her daughters cried out: "Help, help. The fox, the fox!" and after him they all ran, the dog, the cow and her calf, the pigs, the ducks and geese. They all chased after the fox and made such a hubbub, the noise resounded throughout the woods. As they approached the fox, Chantecleer just managed to gasp: "Tell them not to bother, tell them you are going to eat me. Tell them to take their noise away."

"Fine!" said the fox, most pleasantly surprised by Chantecleer's advice, "I'll do just as you say."

And, as he opened his mouth, Chantecleer escaped from his jaws and flew, at once, high up into a tree. When the fox saw that the cock was free he pleaded: "Alas, alas, O Chantecleer! So far as I have given you cause for fear by seizing you and carrying you away I have done you wrong, I must admit. But, sir, I did it with no ill intent. Come down, and I shall tell you what I meant."

"No, no," declared Chantecleer. "You will never again persuade me to sing and wink my eyes."

Partelet forgave Chantecleer and never, for the rest of his life, did Chantecleer listen to flattery.

The Frog Prince

Once upon a time there lived a king who had five beautiful daughters, and the youngest was the most beautiful of all. Close to the king's castle lay a great, dark forest and one day the youngest princess decided to walk amongst the trees. She wandered about for some time until, at last, feeling hot and tired, she sat down by the side of a cool well in the forest glade.

In her hand the princess carried a golden ball, a precious gift from her father, and as she rested by the well she threw up the ball and caught it, then she threw it higher and higher until one time, stretching out her hands to the ball, she let it slip through her fingers. It bounced against a tree, then ricocheted off and dropped into the well:

Splash!

The princess peered down into the deep well but

however hard she looked she could not see to the bottom. Tears streamed down her cheeks: "If only I could get my ball back again, I would give away all my fine clothes and my jewels, and everything that I have in the world," she sighed.

While she was sobbing, and speaking her thoughts out loud a frog popped its head out of the water: "Princess, why on earth are you crying, why do you weep so bitterly?" he asked.

The Princess turned around but when she saw the ugly, squat creature, his face raised to hers, she shuddered in disgust: "Mind your own business. What on earth can you do. If you really want to know, my golden ball has fallen into the well."

The frog answered her, in his deep, kindly voice: "I am not interested in your jewels or in your pearls or in any of your fine clothes. What would I do with them? But, dear princess, if you will only love me and let me live with you, and allow me to eat from your golden plate, and sleep upon your bed, I will fetch your ball."

"What silly things he does say," thought the Princess, "how on earth could anyone love such a grotesque, slimy creature. This well is so deep he will never be able to get out of it."

So she turned to face the frog: "Yes, yes, bring me my ball, please. I will do anything you ask of me, I promise."

Without hesitation, the frog plunged into the well, dropping deep, deep down into the water. After a while he emerged, clutching the golden ball which he let fall at the feet of the princess.

The beautiful golden ball! Eagerly, the princess picked up her toy, overjoyed at seeing it once more. She quite forgot to say good-bye to the frog or to thank him. All her thoughts were directed towards the castle as she started to run through the forest.

"Stay, princess, stay and take me with you. You have given me your word, you

have made me a promise," the frog croaked after her, his voice full of sadness. But the princess was deaf to his pleas and ran faster than ever through the darkening forest.

The following day, just as the princess was sitting at the table with the king and all his court, she heard a strange noise:

Tap, Tap, – Tap, Tap.

It was the sound of tiny feet on the cold marble. Something, some creature, was struggling to climb the marble staircase. The sound continued:

Tap, Tap, – Tap, Tap.

Soon there was a gentle knock at the door and a sad croaky voice called out:

"Open the door, my princess dear,
Open the door to thy true love here!
And mind the words that thou and I said
By the fountain cool in the greenwood shade."

The princess leapt from the table, ran to the door and opened it. There, at her feet, was the quite forgotten frog. She was most terribly frightened. She banged the door shut and returned to the table feeling quite unwell.

"Why do you look so pale, my dear? What has happened?" the King enquired kindly.

"Oh," she answered, trying hard to disguise her feelings, "it is only a slimy frog who just happened to lift my ball out of the water. I sort of made a promise to him that he might live with me here. Truly, I never believed that he would be able to climb out of that deep, slippery well. I wasn't making a *true* promise. Now he is at the door and he wants to come in."

The frog knocked again, most gently, and sounding even more forlorn than before, repeated his request.

"Open the door, my princess dear,
Open the door to thy true love here!

And mind the words that thou and I said
By the fountain cool in the greenwood shade."

The king listened intently to his words and then turned to the young princess: "As you have made this promise, you must keep it. Go to the door and welcome this kind frog who helped you in your time of need."

The Princess hesitated. She slowly opened the door and the frog hopped quietly into the room and followed her to the table: "Pray lift me upon a chair," he said to the princess, "and allow me to sit next to you." The princess did as he asked and then the frog said: "Put your plate closer to me that I may eat out of it." She pushed her plate towards him and when he had eaten as much as he could, he croaked: "Now I feel so tired; carry me upstairs and put me into your little bed."

And the Princess took him up in her hand and placed him upon the pillow of her own bed where he slept all night long. As soon as it was light, he jumped up, hopped down stairs, and out of the castle. "He is gone at last," thought the princess, "now I shall be troubled no more."

But she was mistaken, for when night came she heard the familiar noise:
Tap, Tap, – Tap, Tap.

Reluctantly, she approached her bedroom door and opened it. The frog hopped in and slept upon her pillow as before.

On the third night the princess was drifting off to sleep when she heard the now familiar sound:

Tap, Tap, – Tap, Tap.

and the frog once more claimed his place on the pillow of the princess. But the following morning she was astonished to find, not the frog squatting on her pillow, but a handsome prince standing at the head of her bed.

The prince's story was a long and sad one. He related to the princess how he had been enchanted by a malicious fairy, who had changed him into the form of a frog, a form in which he was fated to remain until a princess should take him out of the well and let him sleep upon her bed for three nights.

"You," continued the prince, "have broken this cruel charm, and now I have nothing to wish for but to ask you to come with me into my father's kingdom where I will marry you, and love you as long as you live."

The young princess, you may be sure, was not long in giving her consent and as they spoke a splendid carriage drove up with eight beautiful horses decked with plumes of feathers and golden harness. Behind the carriage rode the prince's servant, the faithful Henry and they all set out, full of joy, for the Prince's kingdom.

After a long journey they reached the end of their destination and there they were married. Much feasting and rejoicing took place and the frog prince and his princess lived happily for the rest of their lives.

A Lion and a Mouse

Once upon a time a lion was walking through the jungle. He was the king of the beasts and all the animals were frightened of him and stood in awe of him. It happened that very day that a small mouse had built his nest directly in the lion's path and the lion stepped on the nest,

squashing the mouse under his
paw. When the lion felt the mouse
wriggling underneath his paw he was angry and thought he
would gobble up the mouse for his supper. But the mouse
asked him if he would kindly spare his life and, because the lion didn't
feel very hungry, he let the mouse go on his way.

Two or three days later, the same lion was lured into a trap, caught in
a hunter's snare. He bellowed for help but none of the beasts of the forest
came near him. However, the same mouse whose life he had spared just
two or three days before, heard the roaring lion and ran to see what was
the matter. When he saw that the lion was trapped, he jumped up on the
lion's back and ran along the rope of the snare. Then he bit his way
through the rope and the lion went free.

And the moral of this story is that if you do a good deed for somebody
that same person will often help when you
yourself are in need of assistance.

The Bear and the Bees

Once upon a time there was rather a foolish bear who was walking through a wood. It was a very hot day and the bear lay down under a tree and went to sleep. While he was sleeping a bee came and buzzed around his nose. He swatted at the bee with his paw and the bee was so frightened he stung the bear right on his nose.

The bear was furious. He got up, charged into the bee garden and, without stopping to think, he kicked over all the beehives in furious revenge. This made the bees very angry. They flew at the bear and stung him in a thousand places, so that he was forced to run away, wishing that he had never gone near them at all.

And the moral of this story is that it is foolish to try and get revenge for one small injury if by doing so you make hundreds of enemies.